Sam

Ranjit

Molly

Natalie

Martin

Carl

Our Class

William

Lily

Stories by Rose Impey   Pictures by Sue Porter

Theresa

ORCHARD BOOKS

Victoria

Tammy

Thomas

Jon

Matthew

Rebecca

Austin

Sally

Susie

For two First Class teachers,
Diana Mackey and Kate Markless.

ORCHARD BOOKS
96 Leonard Street
London EC2A 4XD
Orchard Books Australia
Unit 31/56 O'Riordan Street, Alexandria, NSW 2015
ISBN 1 84121 668 2
First published in Great Britain in 1992
This edition published in 2001
Text © Rose Impey 1992
Illustrations © Sue Porter 1992 and 2001; interior designed by Sue Porter for Orchard Books
The rights of Rose Impey to be identified as the author and of Sue Porter to be
identified as the illustrator have been asserted by them in accordance with the
Copyright, Designs and Patents Act, 1988.
A CIP catalogue record for this book is available from the British Library.
1 3 5 7 9 10 8 6 4 2
Printed in Belgium

Contents

Experiments

Mrs Candy's Story

In Mrs Candy's class the children
paint pictures, write stories and read books.
Also they do experiments.

They plant seeds to find out
if they grow better in dark cupboards
or on window-sills.

"This one's mine," says Martin. "It's the biggest."
"It's got my name on," says Natalie.

They try to recognise things
with their eyes closed.

"Mrs Candy," says Susie, "Matthew's being
very silly."
"Matthew," says Mrs Candy.
"I was only using my senses," says Matthew.

They do experiments with magnets
and light bulbs and candles.
Every day they learn something new.

Sometimes the children make up
their own experiments. They try to find out
how many books it takes to reach the ceiling.
"Nearly there!" says Theresa.
"Careful!" says Tammy.

careful!

more books

"That's not what books are for,"
says Mrs Candy.

"I bet my jug holds more than your cup," says Austin.

"Look out," says Jon.

"I'm wet through," says Victoria.

"I wonder what it feels like to stroke a goldfish," says Ranjit.

"Wet," says Lily. "And it tickles."

Carl does an experiment where he cuts the tail off Sally's worm.

"I made that worm for my mum," says Sally.

"I wanted to see if it would grow again," says Carl.

"It better," says Sally.

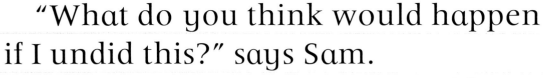

"What do you think would happen if I undid this?" says Sam.

"Let's experiment," says David.
Thomas watches. He smiles.

"Mrs Candy, Mrs Candy, come quick," calls David.

"What a mess!" says Mrs Candy.

"It was an experiment," says Sam.
Sometimes experiments end in tears.

Mrs Candy's class love science.
Every day they learn something new.
So does Mrs Candy.

The Biggest and the Best

Martin's Story

Whatever Martin does
it has to be the biggest and the best.
And Martin likes to do it first.

Martin and Jon play a game.
Martin has four boards; Jon has one.
"I won!" says Martin.
"I think you cheated," says Jon.

the winner!

9

Martin and Victoria do their sums.
"I finished first," says Martin. "I won."
"It isn't a race," says Victoria.

The children on Martin's table make models.
All the time Martin calls out, "Mrs Candy,
Mrs Candy. Mine's the best."
"They're all nice," says Mrs Candy.

When the class line up for PE, Mrs Candy says, "Find a partner and walk in twos. *No running.*"
But Martin likes to be first.
"Don't push," says Sally.

In the hall Martin climbs highest, runs fastest, jumps furthest and catches the most balls.
"Look at me!" he calls, over and over again.
"Be careful," says Mrs Candy.

All afternoon Martin builds a tower.

"This is going to be the biggest, most gigantic tower in the whole, wide world," he says.
"In the entire universe actually. *Look everybody!*"

"Whoops! Sorry!" says Sam.
"*Oh, dear,*" says Mrs Candy.
But Martin doesn't cry.
"I don't mind," he says.
"I think Martin is the bravest boy in the class," says Mrs Candy.
"In the entire school actually."

Dracula's Daughter

Natalie's Story

Natalie's mum has a new baby.
She has breakfast in bed.
A piece of toast and a glass of tomato juice.
   "Looks like blood," says Natalie.
   "Dracula's breakfast," says Dad.
   "Delicious," says Dracula.
   "Yuk," says Natalie.

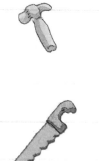

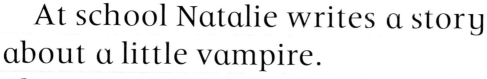

At school Natalie writes a story about a little vampire.
She paints a picture, red all over.
"Lots and lots of blood," she says.
"Oh, dear," says Mrs Candy.

Natalie plays hospitals with Jon.
First she mends his broken arm.
Then she pretends to cut off his leg.
Then she gives him a new heart.
"Now I want to be the doctor," says Jon.

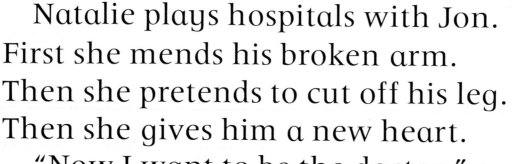

Later Natalie plays at dentists.

"I'm going to take Baby's tooth out," she says.

"Baby hasn't got any teeth yet," says Sally.

"Just pretend," says Natalie.

Baby pretends it hurts. She cries loudly.

At dinnertime Sam bumps into David.

Now David has a wobbly tooth.

He doesn't like the feel of it.

"I can pull it out," says Natalie.

15

"Sit in the dentist's chair," she says.
David doesn't feel a thing.
"Look, Natalie pulled it out," he tells the teacher.
"Take it home for the tooth fairy," she says.

Later Martin has a wobbly tooth.
So does Thomas.
Then Lily thinks her tooth feels loose too.
Natalie pulls them all out.

Soon half the class want their teeth pulling out.
"What's going on here?" asks the teacher.
"We're going to the dentist," says Carl.
"Oh, Natalie!" says Mrs Candy.
"You are bloodthirsty today."
Natalie grins. "I'm Dracula's daughter," she says.

17

Slow Down, Sam

Sam's Story

Sam was always in a hurry.
She couldn't *wait* for Christmas,
to go on her holidays, to open her presents.
Most of all, Sam couldn't wait to start school.
On the first day Mum said,
"Be a good girl, do as you're told and Sam
. . . *slow down.*"

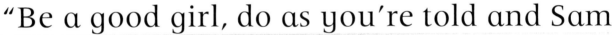

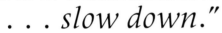

What are you doing?

First Mrs Candy said,
"Write your name on your book,
then go over it with felt pen."
Sam went over it – *all* over it.
"Now you can't read it," said Victoria.

Then Mrs Candy said,
"Everyone get undressed for PE.
Quickly, please."
Sam got undressed – completely undressed.
"Not all your clothes, sweetheart,"
said the teacher. David giggled.
"That'll do," said Mrs Candy.

When Mrs Candy said that Sam could play
with the water *or* the sand, Sam did both.
"What a mess," said Sally.
Mrs Candy said, "Sam, come here!"
"Now," said the teacher, "just . . . *slow down*."

At break Sam played at skipping

and football

and Batman

and kiss-chase

and aliens from outer space.

At dinnertime she played at handstands

and catching

and doctors and nurses

and "What time is it, Mr Wolf?"

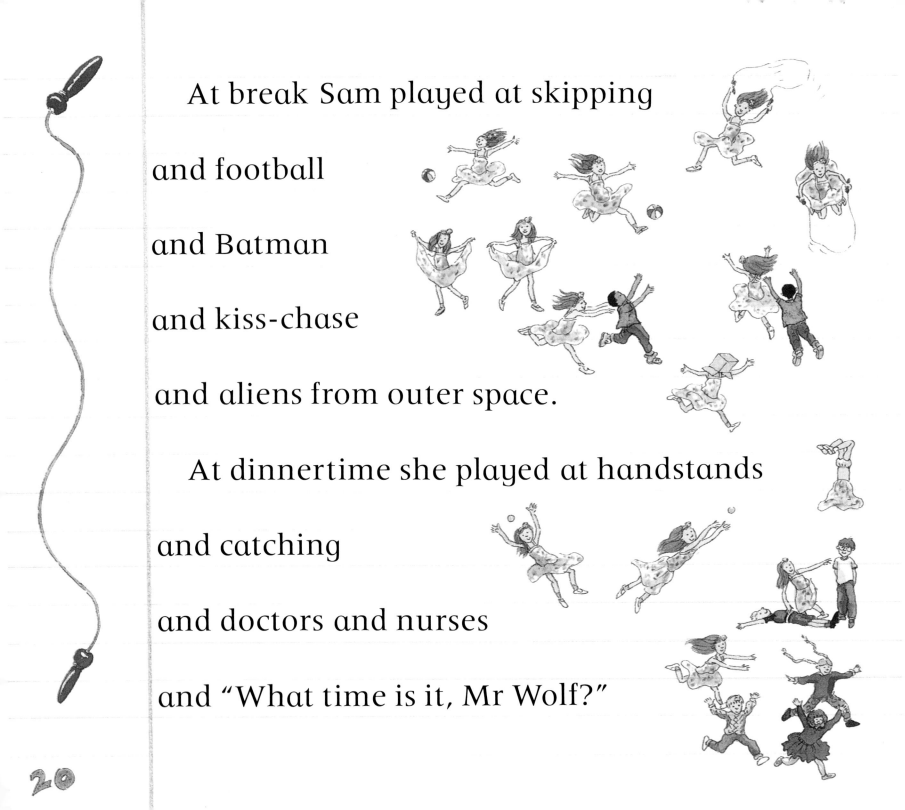

And in the afternoon . . . Sam slowed down.
She lay on the bed in the Home Corner.
She tried to have a nap.

"Wake up," said Natalie.
"You have to look after the baby."

At hometime Mum came to collect Sam.
"Hello, lovely," she said, "did you like school?"
"It was okay," said Sam, yawning,
"but I don't think I'll go again."

The Wanderer

Ranjit's Story

When Ranjit was a baby
he was always wandering off.
When he was two they
found him in the park,
half a mile away.

When he was three
he disappeared on holiday.
Everyone was worried, except Ranjit.
He wasn't lost; he was exploring.

When Ranjit started school
his mum said, "Mrs Candy,
keep your eye on my boy.
He's a wanderer."

And he was. He was always missing.
"Ranjit's gone again, Miss," said Victoria.
They found him in the boiler room,
talking to the caretaker's cat.
Ranjit wasn't lost; he was exploring.

Once Ranjit set off home
in the middle of the morning,
"We were so worried," said Mrs Candy.
"I was going to see my grandma," said Ranjit.

23

In the spring Mrs Candy's class
went on a trip to the zoo.

"Now remember," said the teacher,
"don't feed the animals,
don't put your fingers near the bars
and don't wander off."

The children looked at lots of animals.
Ranjit liked the ducks best.
He followed them all along the path,
past the anteaters, past the monkeys,
past the flamingoes.

Suddenly Ranjit stopped.
There was no one in sight.
He looked up . . . and up . . . and up.
There was the most enormous elephant.
  "I want my mummy!" he cried.

But Mrs Candy had sent out a search party.
"Here he is," said Sam.
"I saw him first," said Martin.
"I was so worried," said Mrs Candy.
And this time Ranjit said . . . ."So was I."

Frogman's Mother

David's Story

When David had a new T-shirt
he wouldn't take it off.
He even went to bed in it.

When David had a new satchel
he wore it all day.
"Frogma-a-an," he said,
over and over again.

"You can be Freddie," he told his sister.
"I'll be Frogman . . ."
"What about me?" said Mum.
"You can be Frogman's mother."

27

At school David painted a picture and made a model and wrote a story.

"Can't you think of anything else?" said Mrs Candy.

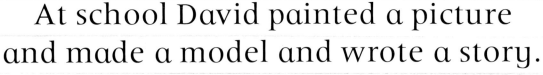

Some of the children were dressing up. The teacher said, "What would you like to be when you grow up?"

"A policeman," said Carl.

"A fireman," said Natalie.

"Frogman, Hero of the Deep," said David.

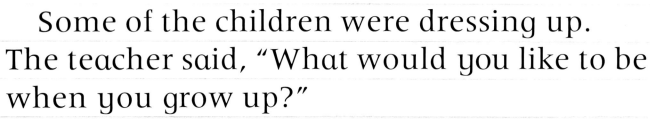

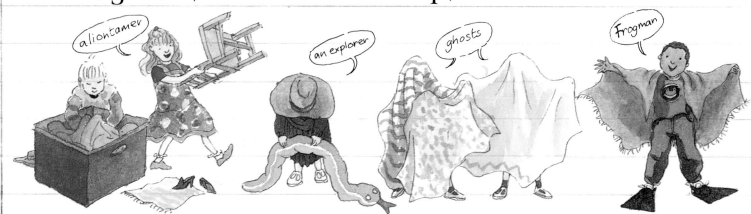

"Let's make a graph," said Mrs Candy, "to show how we all get to school."
"I walk," said Sally.
"By bus," said Martin.
"On the Froghopper," said David.

Frogman

In assembly the children said prayers for different people.
"The Queen," said Susie.
"The Prime Minister," said Jon.
"Frogma-a-an," said David.

"I think *you're* being silly," said the teacher.
"We don't want to hear any more about Frogman,
thank you very much."
David went quiet.
He didn't speak again all morning.

At lunchtime, when Mrs Candy
asked the children who made their packed lunches,
Victoria said, "My daddy."
Ranjit said, "My grandma."
David said nothing.

So Mrs Candy said,
"Who made your lunch, David?"
David grinned. "Frogman's mother," he said.
"Rivet, rivet, rivet, rivet, Frogma-a-an."

In Mrs Candy's class the children paint pictures,
write stories and read books.
Every day they learn something new . . .

And so does Mrs Candy.